The Wilderness, Berkhamsted, Hertfordshire, HP4 2AZ, UK.
501 Nelson Place, P.O. Box 141000, Nashville, TN 37214-1000, USA.

Written by Rosie Greening.
Illustrated by Stuart Lynch.

We are the grOOvicOrns!

ROSIE GREENING ★ STUART LYNCH

make
believe
ideas

Everyone **loves** unicorns. They always make a fuss. But you know who **should** be famous?

I ♥ unicorns!

The unicorns make **rainbows**
that **curve** from side to side.

but they make
amazing
slides!

Unicorns sign **hOOfprints,**

My Unicorn Scrapbook

To Rabbit,
Love
Glitter

and they grant your WISHES, too.

HAPPY BIRTHDAY

We don't have
magic powers,

Buckinghorn Palace

We have **MULTICOLOreD** tents

All Welcome

The unicorns **bring SunShine** everywhere they go.

The sun is **super boring.**
You know what's better?

SNOW!

The unicorns are bigheads — they **SHOW OFF** all day long.

Glow 'n' go
hoof polish

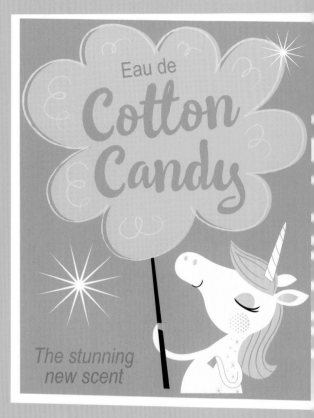

Eau de Cotton Candy

The stunning new scent

Who would want to smell like cotton candy?

The snooty unicorns, that's who!

They **never** want to play with us, and —

HEY!

You've got it wrong.

Mane-gain!

Grow luscious locks in minutes

They're not THAT bad . . .

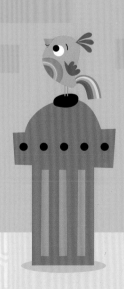

It's **hard** to be a **unicorn** – we have a **lot** to do.

There's **never** any time to play. We wish we were like **YOU!**

To Do

Make rainbow
*
Grant wish
*
Rainbow school
*
Hoofprint signing
*
Mane maintenance
*
Polish hooves
*
Attend premiere

Everyone is different,
but **special** in their way.

So let's **learn** from one another
and have more **fun** every day!